An Indoor Kind of Girl

An Indoor Kind of Girl
© 2018 Frankie Barnet

ISBN 978-0-9939464-9-3

Published by Metatron Press
Montreal Québec
www.metatron.press

First edition
Third printing

Cover art and design | Louise Reimer

We acknowledge the support of the Canada Council for the Arts,
which last year invested $153 million to bring the arts to Canadians
throughout the country.

Canada Council   Conseil des arts
for the Arts   du Canada

AN INDOOR
KIND OF GIRL

FRANKIE BARNET

Metatron
Montreal

Contents

Gay for Her

First you meet her at a potluck, that girl from the party. Kara's house? Yeah, that girl with the nachos. Or maybe you meet her in the eighth grade. She remembers you vaguely from high school, mistaking you for someone named Bethany, but no hard feelings, it's all super chill.

She isn't as pretty as you or maybe she is much, much prettier than you and you ask your friends, do you think she's pretty? They tell you that she looks kinda like Scarlett Johansson, but that's only from certain angles and from certain other angles, she looks like Al Pacino.

It's your 337th time drinking alcohol. It's your fifth time smoking weed today. It's her DJ night and maybe it's the night you sleep with Brian, the person that of all people you've slept with in your so-far life you regret sleeping with the most. You sit across the table from her, she's wearing velour. Never in your life have you heard anyone talk so explicitly about masturbating with the bathroom faucet. You think, *I'm going to add her on Facebook.* This very tall girl.

Find out she is also a vegetarian. She'll tell you she hates vegetarians. You type back, "Lol me too." Skip the assigned readings for class, hang out just the two of you and go for Chinese. Hang out just the two of you and get totally wasted. "Borrow" a sweater. You both have the same first name.

Weird she's had sex with so many more people than you have. Weird that you've had sex with so many more people than she has. Weird that you've slept with exactly the same amount of people, what a funny coincidence. The both of you in stitches over Brian's penis. You've been called a "fuck puppet," she's been called a "cum bucket." Refer to her with other people and her last name is dropped, simply Lisa, simply Jess, simply Marianna.

You tell her something about your mother that applies directly to how she feels about her mother, and then she tells you something about her ex-boyfriend that applies directly to how you feel about your family's late Bichon. See her cry for the first time. She sees you cry, like, every day. You have completely different names.

You write in your diary, "I love her, but I am not in love with her."

You look at her and wonder how you've never noticed before that she is insanely pretty. It's in the curve of her nose, or it's in-between her nose and her mouth and it's her ears and toes and the way she just gets you. She's so pretty, and she's your best friend, of course she is, who else in the world would be your best friend? You promise always to be friends, even when you are older. You promise to always smoke weed.

There's free cake in the Women's Studies department to celebrate Simone de Beauvoir's birthday. You sneak in and talk about how hard you are falling in love with Brian. She tells you it's in the stars, she says she'd kill for your stars.

You promise you are not mad she didn't make it Friday and you promise you will make it Tuesday. You are late for her birthday dinner. You are late for her birthday party. But you're right there at her vernissage when she spends the whole night talking to her art friends, the ones with weird hair who never acknowledge you, so you hang out near the back and drink the cheap wine alone.

Google Simone de Beauvoir when you get home, feeling guilty over pizza. *Oh well I'm prettier than that!* Measuring your thighs with your hands cupped together.

You've been feeling uneasy lately with the way you feel in the mornings after smoking weed, so you decide to take a little break, just until you feel more balanced again. It's the year she decides to get real about her pottery. She moves to St. Henri and says she wants to be a lawyer. She moves to Calgary to learn massage. She's always bragging about her art friends and what blogs they run. She's always bragging about her boyfriend and the time his parents met Obama. She's great at school and she's great at the drums. She looks like Kim Kardashian, she looks like Sky Ferreira and she looks like Kourtney Kardashian. She's great at dressing herself, she rules at sucking dick, and she just inherited ten thousand dollars from her grandfather. She is so much better than you at everything. It's like she is your younger brother, who your parents have always liked more, and then she goes out to the bar and she sucks your younger brother's dick.

You're really so smart. You're really so nice, so unappreciated, really. You sleep with her ex-boyfriend. The night you sleep with her sociology professor. The night she doesn't even text you back. So lame. She is so lame, you can do better. You sleep with that guy who works at the Chinese place, but do not tell her, or anyone, about it ever, because you find out later that he is seventeen.

She starts acting like she can do better than you, and you in turn become certain you can do better than her, because what kind of person would think they can do better than their best friend? Only a sad and miserable person with a sad and miserable life would ever want to implement hierarchies like that. Who does she think she is, to tell you that you have a drinking problem? Even if she was the one who introduced you to Brian.

Play out fantasies in your head where you're finally honest about how pathetic she's become. Fantasies where you gently let her know how hopeless her Nutrition degree is. You start to make jokes with other friends, jokes about her improv and her weird dad.

"There is a new sense of freedom in my life, I can feel it," you write in your diary, when you're barely even thinking about her. You meet new people and talk about new things, better, smarter things, cooler things, things that have more to do with music and Palestine. You run into her one day at a party and nod from across the room, then artfully avoid each other, like she's just some guy you once fucked in a bathroom somewhere.

One day remember that time you went with your friend to the Women's Studies department and ate that free cake. You sat on the couch and she explained to you who Simone de Beauvoir was. You think, she really was very smart.

That night or a week later, get blackout drunk and think about how unhappy with your life you are. How tired you are of so many of the things you've chosen to define yourself by. Why on earth did you cut your bangs like that? Girls like you are becoming lawyers, girls like you have at least been to Europe. All you have is your stupid fucking haircut. If only you could just lose fifteen pounds, or maybe you should never have broken up with Brian.

Sit at your computer or in front of a piece of paper, maybe even the back side of a list you wrote of ways to get in shape. Remember that time you got drunk in the park with your friend and made fun of all the dogs. When she peed the bed in New York City. She removed your plantar warts the day after Halloween while watching *Maid in Manhattan*. Will you ever have a friend like that again? And you do not fully understand what happened between the two of you. Maybe you can see how the way you acted towards her could have been misconstrued to make her think you didn't really care about or love her, but you only meant it that way because you were angry, or jealous, or insecure, or actually a muddled confusion of all of these things and more, which you never expected to get so out of hand. "Why were you so hard on me?" you ask her. "I don't know why I was so hard on you," you tell her. You tell her, "I miss you." You tell her about how lonely you feel, now that she is not your friend anymore.

Wake up in the morning, already late for work. Wake up in the afternoon and puke for the rest of the day. Remember vaguely drawing a picture? Remember typing something up, but when you check your computer, there isn't anything there because halfway through you realized how uncool it all sounded, like you're gay for her or something, and plus she's the one who should be doing the apologizing. Wake up in the morning and don't remember anything at all. There you are in the bathroom, over the toilet, struggling to believe something as neon as bile could come from inside of your body.

You do not remember anything, you do not say anything, until the next time you get blackout drunk, tomorrow or a week later, when you write, do not send and then delete another email about your feelings towards her, but you don't remember that either, so it is more like you do not feel anything, and have no confusion whatsoever.

Cherry Sun

You could tell the animal wasn't interested in mating season, she'd gone to great lengths to make that obvious. But this was a business and babies were what the people wanted to see. Come spring, teachers, carpenters, musicians, poets and lawyers visited our zoo, paid twelve-fifty and stared at all the babies. How thrilling, to be in the presence of such fresh life, such big eyes and awkward gaits.

First, there were problems with her hormones, then her temperature. The vet was called in, spread her hide taut then pricked her with his potions. "She'll be fine now," he said, "I've got her all balanced out."

Her name was Nala and she was a capybara. "I know you don't want to do it," I told her, because at this point I was levelling with her. I wasn't feeding her any of the bullshit I saw other keepers feed their animals. To the seals: *But you'll totally outshine the walruses in the afternoon show!* To the Siberian tiger: *Here are some messages from your family in the wild!*

"Although," I told her, "it might not be as important as you think it is. Just because you have sex with a guy doesn't mean it explains everything about you. It's the twenty-first century. You can have sex with whoever you want, it doesn't matter."

We'd all been there, or at least I had. More times than I'd care to admit. Oh, I'd fucked all those guys: the chimpanzee guy, the sloth bear guy, the guy who ran the cafeteria. These days nobody expected you to be in love.

I told her about the guy I had just started seeing, who minded the antelopes. Actually, he had this nervous way about him, a habit of always knowing how much each keeper's animal was worth in parts and then treating them accordingly. "It's not like I'm coming," I told Nala, just to manage any expectation she might have had. "I mean, sometimes it can hurt, he gets pretty rough down there but...well, I could take it as a compliment really, that he needs me so hard like that."

There were seven capybaras, including Raja, the stud. Their pen was a struggling exhibit in the small mammals department, consistently overshadowed by the meerkats. We had given them pretty much anything they could have wanted: lettuce, water, some shrubs for shade, but they remained awful at performing for the visitors. "We all know you're related to the rat," we told them, "but it's nothing to be ashamed of. All of us have shameful aspects to our family history." But those giant vermin were just so stubborn. If we hadn't gotten the idea to throw their food along the viewing window, the animals would hardly have gotten up from chewing their bark at all.

A team of three handled the rodents: a grad student doing her practicum, a recent high school dropout who happened to be related to the mayor, and myself. Like I said, we were struggling. What killed us was that the meerkats were even more like the rat (considering the tail and all) and yet it didn't seem to bother them as a species at all. The meerkats had *The Lion King* and it had gone to their heads. They were always dancing around, popping out of holes like they had just discovered new air. I'd seen people actually cheer.

The capybaras were a different story. Generally, what happened was about five minutes after finding out what a capybara was, the novelty was gone. It was a zoo after all, there were lions, tigers, hot dogs wrapped in bacon.

In the wild, capybaras often ate, slept and copulated in the water. In the zoo, because of our limited resources, we borrowed a plastic tub from the seal guy to induce intimacy. The mares floated noses up while Raja treaded behind them with his front paws resting on their haunches.

"You ever done it in water?" asked the seal guy, whose condition for lending us the tub was that he was allowed to watch.

"Yeah," I lied, "I've done it everywhere."

Raja was usually good to impregnate two mares a day, three if we pushed him. We needed to have all of the mares impregnated that week, before Raja left on a road trip through the midwest, to impregnate mares in Calgary, Minnesota, Indianapolis and Chicago. What we wanted was for the pups to emerge *en masse*, wet, big eyed and adorable.

But Nala wouldn't fuck him. When we put her in the water, she dove to the bottom of the pool and kicked Raja in the face after he dove after her.

"This is what you have to do," said our superiors, who gave us a demonstration in their executive office using two plush otters from the gift store. Alright, I thought. Simple enough and for a good cause.

Though in real life, when I stood at the edge of the pool holding her front legs and the mayor's niece tugged a rope that harnessed both her back legs, it was much more difficult.

"This is fucked, this is fucked, this so fucked up," muttered the grad student under her breath as the three of us listened to the violent, splashing water.

"Listen," I said to Nala when we had a moment alone. "I know you're nervous. But what you need to understand is that all we want from you is to be happy and healthy. You get to have three babies! Aren't you excited?"

She looked at me.

"Yeah, three of them! How does it feel?" I really was curious, and a little drunk, from the tequila I'd snuck in for lunch.

She buried her head in the dirt, like she was trying to prove that the dirt went all the way down to the earth's core, not that she knew what a core was, not that it wasn't just the cement pool where the dolphins lived, then died, that one record-breaking winter.

"Clarice!" That was the grad student, always on my ass. "Who are you talking to? No cell phones!"

As I stood up, I turned to say one more thing to Nala. "You can't just stop eating," I said. "You've got to start taking better care of yourself." And for a little while, she did.

When a baby was born at the zoo, you could feel it in the air. When a baby was born, everyone was allowed to abandon their posts to watch. We all crowded around the new mother and melted as she licked the afterbirth from her fresh young. Usually one of the small monkeys girls said something like, "Oh my god I can feel it in my ovaries!" as the elephant guys shifted away from her nervously. A representative from the executive office would come to visit and name the new being with a megaphone. Welcome Simba, welcome Nemo, welcome Pluto, welcome Roo.

What was with the babies in this place? What was with the people lining pits and cages every Saturday afternoon, pointing at shadows thinking it might be a baby. There were babies on billboards, babies on the side of buses. People hung them on their backs like a jacket, or on their fronts like a medallion. They gave them names and picked out clothes for them to wear. A baby had the potential to be anything and anything had the potential to be a baby, when you were desperate to see one in the snow leopard's cage.

Five months later, our mares writhed in the dirt and the sacs of their young burst forth slimy and pungent. We had put Nala through so much, yet watching her with the little ones it became clear we had made the right decision. It was a series of right decisions that led us to this moment. She slurped embryonic sac from their tiny faces. Hers were the smallest and therefore cutest ones. It was beautiful and peaceful, and I felt like I was too, just by being near them. I swigged some of the tequila I'd hid in my backpack, holding my stomach together as it sizzled. I didn't always drink at work, but when I did, it was usually in slim mickeys, which I hid in the waistband of my skirt. I wondered, briefly, how incredible it would feel to be them, somehow all four of them.

The antelope guy, who had lately been acting distant, texted me on his break and I snuck out to meet him in the secluded shadows between Penguin Plunge and the Amphibian House.

He reached his hand under my skirt and found the mickey, laughed and rolled his eyes. "Crazy, crazy, Clarice." He was shaking his head, then unscrewed the cap and took a deep swig without even asking.

"Hey!"

"What?" He looked at me and swigged again, then threw the bottle onto a bench. "I'm going to make it up to you." He started kissing my neck and moving lower.

I wanted him to lick me more. "Harder," I said, but that wasn't it necessarily. "Slower," but it wasn't that either.

What was meant to happen was that he licked me all up. My outside disappeared and for a great flash I was just my inside. It happened sometimes, like with the sloth bear guy when I said, "Oh god."

With the guy from the cafeteria when I said, "Heeeeeahhhhhhh."

The antelope guy took his penis out, flipped me around, and pushed himself into me. It felt so big at first, but it was just like a shot. Only for a second, then almost nothing.

When we finished the antelope guy said, "Have I ever told you that you have a real seventies bush?" even though he had told me many times.

I walked back to the capybaras feeling loose and fuzzy. The grad student was deep in conversation with the veterinarian. "This better not mean we lose our bonuses!" the mayor's niece said. "I need that bonus!" She stormed past me. The grad student sighed deeply, like a man. What had happened, the veterinarian explained, was that Nala's pups, all three of them, turned out to have been dead. They had been dead for some time, he told me, which explained their underdevelopment. "It's actually not un-common," he said, "when an animal's under stress."

Before I knew it, my shift was over and the zoo was closed. I could have gone home, I could have just left and eaten chips in my room, watching something stupid on TV. Even though I lived right across the river, it took almost forty-five minutes with the bus over the nearest bridge. Sometimes I joked to myself, just swim. Just swim, I told myself, and on that day for some reason I really felt like it. But then what? Show up for dinner completely soaked and say what to my parents?

So I stayed with the capybaras, I sat beside their feeding gate and watched Nala in the setting, cherry sun. She was up and walking, which was strange. Weren't there tests? Shouldn't there be tests? I thought. She was walking away from the south wall of the pen.

"So you're pleased with yourself then? So with the babies, that was all just for show?"

She stopped about five feet away from the wall and turned around.

"Well congratulations." I took another swig of the tequila, the last one. "You got rid of your babies, all of your babies are dead."

The light was really like grenadine. It washed over Nala and the other capybaras, west of her in the pen, resting quietly and chewing on whatever shit we'd given them to chew on.

I thought about the time I had sex with my humanities teacher in high school. When I got stoned and drove over his lawn. "You're crazy Clarice," he told me. "You're acting crazy!"

"Allan! Allan!" I said. That was his name. Whenever I said it, I made a point to pronounce both the L's.

Nala had her eyes glued ahead of her, and I watched as she flung herself into motion, sprinting forward headfirst. She bounced off of the wall, landing with a heavy thud on the dirt and straw. Then she got up, paced back and ran again.

"What are you doing?" I asked Nala. "What are you even doing with your life?"

But she just kept throwing herself against that wall. She threw herself against the wall over and over again, so many times that the blood overtook her tiny body and at the end of the week, she was incinerated with her children and several tropical fish.

It Is Often the Beautiful Ones You Have to Watch Out For

This was the year Beyoncé wore a dress made entirely from the sounds of thunder and lightning. From the couch The Painter, with his daughter and wife, watched the beautiful woman on the television screen accept a Grammy Award.

"I want to be her," said his daughter.

"You want to be a singer?" asked his wife.

"No," she said, "I want to cease to exist. I wish that my life had never begun and my soul could occupy that body instead of my own. I wish this," she pinched the skin of her tiny arm, "wasn't even real. And I lived in there." She pointed towards the television: all of the beautiful, shiny people.

She was only twelve, but times had been tough. Money was a problem. They sat on a worn couch the Painter's brother had given them after his hamster had died inside of it. But things were about to change.

"Things are going to get better for us," the Painter told his daughter. "I'm painting a mural."

The mural was to celebrate the history of the town. To be painted on the mural were the man who built the park, the first mayor, and several war veterans from Korea. To be painted was the woman who built the animal shelter, the man who started the music camp for kids, the woman who donated all of the horses.

The Painter even painted his friend, the owner of the auto shop, who had also started the football program at the high school. *Would he ever paint me back?* the Painter wondered as he painted all of the Coach: his lips, chest, even penis, though it was covered by gym shorts.

The Painter and his wife were able to afford a weekend at the shore. They redecorated their modest house. The Painter's wife hung some of his work, so that a painting he had done of the backyard hung in the kitchen, a painting of the bathroom hung in the living room and a painting of their daughter's room hung in the basement. It was to remind them, she said, "How we are all connected."

"Please paint Steve Jobs," someone wrote to the Painter in an email.

"You should be painting what's going on in Lebanon," someone else told him.

"Can you paint my mom for her birthday?"

From their experiences, joys and defeats, everyone in the town had developed their own unique perspectives on life and wanted these reflected in the mural.

The Painter went for beers with the Coach and said, "I think my daughter hates me, I'm almost positive."

Doo-Wop (That Thing) was playing on an old juke-box in the background and the Coach nodded.

"What if I just read her diary?" asked the Painter. "Just to know a little bit about why."

"You can't be doing that," said the Coach. "That's just not something you should be doing."

The Painter's daughter had begun wearing makeup and shirts made from tiny, sparkling triangles. She said that she hated her life and that she wished she had never been born and that the Painter should get a real job.

One day, the Painter was picking out Chinese food in the kitchen when his wife called him from the TV room. "Get in here," she said, "you have to see this!"

A story had surfaced that the Coach had acted inappropriately with a woman. The woman spoke to the newspaper and described how the Coach forced himself on her, once while they were out for drinks at a bar, not in their town, but two towns over, a place known for its nightlife.

Well, what were they doing there? said the townspeople. And the Coach admitted to it, at least partially: "Yes," he said in an official statement sent to the same newspaper, "I have strayed from my marriage."

And what man did not feel the temptation of temptation from time to time? As for the Painter, he thought of Beyoncé on the television, how the buckling atmospheric crack hugged her hips. Were we not all human beings? There was also the matter of the woman's appearance, which would have been troubling to anyone. Women should try to look more natural, many concurred.

But then another woman told a story. Not that she had been to a bar with the Coach, but to his own house, while his wife was out of town. She was beautiful and much younger than the first woman. *Still*, said the people of the town, *it is often the beautiful ones you have to watch out for.* And after all, she had gone to his house. You don't go to someone's house by accident, that was impossible. Most things in life took hard, hard work. Extended effort and dedication. Those were the values taught by the Coach himself, who had transformed many sons into men. Right then, he was in the process of sending a kid to college on an athletic scholarship for the first time

"They just want our money," said the Coach in a private conversation with the Painter, though the Painter wondered, what money? Was he not a small business owner and volunteer? How much money could he have? It would have been impolite to ask. Their conversation shifted to a more comfortable territory: television. "Besides," the Coach said when he was driving the Painter home, "to tell you a secret, I'm sick."

"It's cancer," confirmed the Coach's wife later in a phone call with the Painter. "I told him, go to the doctor, he never listened. And now this. They're saying it's everywhere."

Everywhere? thought the Painter. "We're here for anything you need," said his wife when he handed her the phone.

So it had been inside of him, thought the Painter, for how long? Had it been there when the Painter went to pick up his daughter from school but she was not at school, instead at The Cascades with friends, smoking weed? Or when he saw the Coach and his wife at the supermarket, picking up a rotisserie chicken? The Coach had his arm around his wife in such a proud and confident way that the Painter estimated he had never once touched his own wife comparably. So the Painter returned every item in his basket to its rightful place (the pasta sauce, day-old bread) and bought a rotisserie chicken of his own. He returned home, ate a silent meal with his wife and scowling daughter, only to find out not even two months later that the Coach had been filled with cancer the whole time.

The Coach died and his funeral procession swelled the town. Grown men lined the streets, proud of their tears. That day, the Painter painted a golden halo over the Coach and when he finished, a crowd around him cheered.

Though others had more to say:

"But he raped! And you're saying he's some kind of angel?"

And, "He's not dead, he's probably in Florida somewhere, living it up!"

But still:

"For a man's name to be taken like that, a weak man, at the end of his life? What have we come to, as a town?"

And:

"He did not really rape her, she was his mistress and he released emails that proved it. In the scheme of things, think of all those boys he helped, by uniting the football program?"

Rumors of the Coach's last days had circulated and were whispered into ears with an aura of exclusiveness that was sublime. His fear and withered body.

He was like a leaf, he was like one of those meek leaves you find on the ground in spring after the snow has melted. His last words were a Ghandi quote, no it was a quote from the movie *Rocky*. And he was never afraid, he'd never been afraid of anything, not once in his life. That was why he decided to become an auto mechanic back in high school, kind of like a man vs. machine kind of thing.

Then another woman, though she had not been a woman at the time of the incident she spoke of, gave a statement about the Coach that was leaked to the press. The Painter did not want to read it, but his wife did and summarized it to him one morning in the shower. She had been seventeen.

The Painter knew something had to be done to the mural. So he repainted the Coach as an old man, with the photograph that had run in all the papers, just to put it all out there. Just so no one would be confused, yes, that was the Coach, the one who allegedly assaulted all those women.

But when he finished and looked at the mural from across the street, he knew that whatever idea he thought he had had been lost in translation. If only, he thought, he could use the sounds from the bar that night, the sound of the glass breaking when the Painter tried to illustrate with his hands to the Coach how much he missed his daughter and also the sound of the woman's voice breaking when the reporters swarmed her outside of the news station. Except they were simply not colours of paint the Painter could afford.

"I don't know what to do," he told his wife.

"Honey," she said, "If you listen to everything everybody has to say about your paintings, you'll drive yourself crazy."

"Dad," said his daughter one day after school. "You know that it's true what they're saying about the Coach, right?"

The Painter said that they were very serious accusations, but the Coach had been a great friend to the family, and in the end he had suffered terribly.

"Dad," she said, "I know one of those girls." Which seemed to the Painter improbable because his daughter was only fourteen. Except, he remembered, she was actually sixteen. She was telling him the story of one of her friends, whom the Coach had offered a ride home from school and given a beer to in his car. He invited her into his house for more beer and when he started undressing her and saw that she had her period, he pulled her tampon out of her in order to have sex with her.

"I didn't know what to say when she told me," said his daughter. "I don't think I said the right things."

She was crying now, shaking over his lap. He felt like he was holding some kind of amphibian. He called for his wife.

The Painter went back to the mural and painted the Coach completely naked with drooping wrinkled skin and a penis which, though modelled after his own, was later described as comically shriveled. He did not understand. Why had the Coach needed sex so bad, to do that to such a young girl? Maybe it was true that the Painter did not understand sex, had not understood it his whole life. It was a great painting, and the Painter felt twisted and ashamed for feeling proud of his work at such a time.

They told him it was disgusting, unanimously. After everything the community had been through. With the reporters and the papers and the television shows, after not going to state, now this? It was not something for children to see, it was going to make people sick.

How messed up could you get? The townspeople quickly questioned why the Painter had been given control over the mural in the first place, mounted on the side of the community center.

"In fact," they said, "we hate the community centre." There had been sightings of mice and a rain gutter fell on an aunt's head. Within that context, some argued, the shrivelled penis was actually quite pertinent.

The Painter lost faith in the mural. He did not want to paint for the town anymore, but he did not want another Painter to touch his mural.

By now, he was only painting with his fingers and said to the crowd who watched him that it was to represent how we were all once children. The toes he painted on the mural were as thick as his thumb.

The mayor of the town approached the Painter with sensitivity to his artistic temperament. "It's not that we don't like your new style, but several residents have simply expressed missing your old style."

"We were all kids once," said the Painter, "just lying in bed, looking out the window, wondering about stuff." The Painter had paint all over his hands, his shirt and jeans. Because the Painter had been picking his nose, the midnight paint reached all the way under his nostrils. The paint told no lies.

"I was a kid once," said the mayor later to friends, "and I could paint better than that!"

One day the Painter came home from work and his wife said, "Sweetie, sit down."

"The mural?" he asked.

"Forget about the mural for one second," she said. "My mother had a heart attack."

If he was such a good Painter, then why was he confused? He thought that if he was good enough at painting, he would get into a good school and someone would want to have sex with him there. He wanted to have sex with many girls (even once his sister in a dream) and yet in all of his life, it seemed he had never wanted to have sex as bad as the Coach did, because he had never pulled a tampon out of a sixteen-year-old.

He brought a can of paint and splashed it over the entire mural. "Hey!" said the war veteran.

"What the fuck?" said the descendants of the woman with the horses.

If he booked enough jobs they could go on a honey-moon. If he illustrated enough book covers they could start saving for a baby. If he sold enough paintings the girl could have braces (he did not).

"You don't listen to me," his daughter told him while they argued. "Do you even try to listen to me at all?" Because he made her and she looked just like him, it should have been easy. But instead, she might as well have come from China or grown out of the ground. She said she wanted to become a cardiologist. She said she wanted to go out-of-state. Her boyfriend was twenty-two.

All of the children who had known the Coach began to graduate. The girl he had abused made it to Hollywood Week on *American Idol* and then just hung around L.A. for while. The Painter's daughter bought a dress from Chinatown and wore it to prom with a necklace around her like a belt and when she walked down the stairs of their house, the necklace burst so that the beads fell under the painting of the backyard and into the throat of the brand new used dog. They were cheap plastic pearls. He thought that she would cry, but she laughed and his wife laughed, too. *We're allowed to laugh?* he thought. He looked out the window where the sky was…almost, like the sky needed just one more coat of paint. If he had been a better Painter, then maybe the sky would have been a more clear weather.

It was kind of like years later when his daughter called home from grad school to say that no, she was not going to marry her professor after all, that instead she was going to find herself in India. The Painter's wrist slipped so that the spaghetti fell with the water into the sink, cavernous with the residue of other meals.

Or maybe it was not like that at all, but suddenly his heartbeat was everywhere, bouncing off the walls and coming back to him, like how bats locate one another in the dark.

"If you want to visit me in India," she said, "you can. But there's not going to be any phones or anything."

"Remember how you loved that dress?"

"Dad, there's not going to be any possessions, it's part of the point."

"The one made of all the sounds."

"When I wore the beads around my waist and they snapped?"

"Around the waist was rain, hitting grass. It was very delicate. I remember watching with you. On the television. Do you remember that? Sitting with me?"

"I don't know what you're talking about dad. I have to go."

His wife called from the TV room, was dinner ready?

By now, the rotting community centre had been torn down and rebuilt in the nicer, newly developed neighbourhood of West Point. The mural went with it, dismantled panel by panel then kept, the Painter was told via email, in a municipal storage facility.

What I Was Looking For

At work, a new policy was brought into practice. We were told that from now on, it was integral to say that we were calling from New York City. My job was to sit in front of a computer for nine hours a day, calling businesses across America to offer free credit ratings. Part of the new initiative included talking the part, so, for example, we were instructed to say, "praw-cess-ing" instead of "pro-cessing" like, they told us, the way an American would.

"You need to sound American," my supervisors, a small woman named Emily and a large man named Daryl, said. "No one will want to do business with you unless you're American."

They said that they did not understand us, that what were we, hippies? "Because from the way you pitch," said Daryl, "it's like you don't even want to be making any money." We worked on commission, ten dollars for every credit rating we could convince someone to fax in.

"If I was doing your job," said Emily, "I'd be selling these credit ratings, twenty bucks a piece."

"I had your job," said Daryl, "and I lit up the floor."

Though we were lying, to be honest, I enjoyed it. To live in New York City, I thought. Wow. Just think about that. Some of my friendlier calls would say, "How do you like the big city?" And I would tell them that I could not imagine living anywhere else. Sometimes they would remind me that young women needed to be careful out at night and I assured them that I always was. New York City. Can you imagine?

I think that I was happy during this time. I think I'd say that the only thing really amiss were those turtles, all the little ones living in my apartment.

Supposedly, the turtles came through the pipes, where they lived, made love and reproduced. If this sounds disgusting, then maybe you're used to a higher standard of living than I was, because it really didn't bother me. But they say there's no such thing as one turtle and that's true. Pretty soon I was seeing their little dark green bodies everywhere: on the counters, up next to the wall, and under the tub.

The penalties for harbouring infestationable beings included out-of-province deportation and a fine of up to $750. Every so often you'd hear about a pet rat, or hidden ladybugs. "That's not what Quebec is about," the mayor had said once in an official statement. "What defines us as a province is our impeccable cleanliness." In accordance with city bylaws, your first two infestations of any kind were covered by the landlord, but after that, it became the tenant's responsibility. Unfortunately, I'd had bed bugs and those sparrows who nested in my underwear drawer earlier that year.

"I didn't know that turtles could infest apartments," I had said to the exterminator, who replied that it was not uncommon and then asked me if I was a marine biologist, with a tone and look in his eyes that implied he knew for a fact I was not.

One afternoon at break I returned a call from my cousin Kathy. "It's butterflies," she said, "they're everywhere." Each time my apartment had been fumigated I stayed at hers, so now I couldn't help offering to have her stay at mine.

We were related, but had little in common. She arrived early that evening and we sat down in front of my computer, watching TV and drinking wine. We talked about which wedding dresses we liked on the television show.

"It's funny cause I don't even believe in marriage," Kathy laughed.

"Yeah," I said, even though I didn't care. By that point I'd picked all of the nail polish off of my fingernails, so I began to paint them again, thinking about how I'd be able to pick it all off when I'd finished and they had dried.

"Have you ever been to New York City?" I asked.

She said she had. She said when she was there she met Shia LaBeouf's stunt double for the *Transformers* movies and they had had sex in a TCBY bathroom. "Well," she said, "oral sex."

We finished a bottle of wine and then I ran downstairs to the dep to buy another. When I returned, something in the air had shifted, Kathy stared at me with these long, meaningful looks. "So how *are* you?" she asked when I filled both of our glasses and it occurred to me: She wanted me to talk about Joey, she'd been dying to hear all about it.

"You know," she started, "we were all worried about you, with how much, well you know, with how much you idolized Joey and everything." Well of course, I thought. He was my older brother.

She was drunk and I was drunk, too. I couldn't tell if she was talking with her hands or her mouth. "Isn't death *fucked*?" she said. "There was this girl at my high school you know, and her father had a heart attack on this boat." She took a sip of her wine. Her lips were this deep plum and looked fantastic. "Then she shaved off all her hair and threw it in the river. But the problem was that she was really ugly. So everyone said, what if her hair gets into our water? The stuff we wash ourselves with? It was crazy."

The apartment I lived in was on the second floor of a small house. "We've never had a single turtle before," my landlord had said, suspiciously. But he didn't know me. He didn't know anything about me or where I came from and he had rented me a broken apartment. One that spun. It was spinning now and it had taken Kathy's face with it.

The turtles had been alive on the counters, on the floor along the walls, up against the corner and so forth. So naturally, when I found their bodies afterwards, after the exterminator had failed to remove them, that was where they were. Tiny things, smaller than pill bottles, with the deep green of their skin already souring. Wide open red eyes, staring at something beyond me.

Each time I found a dead body I threw it into a plastic bag and left it outside, in the industrial bin in front of my building. Other times they were not dead, only almost, and I did the same. Other times they were completely alive, moving slowly, towards the sink or the bathtub. Probably, I thought, smelling the water. In total there were four like this, and I kept them secretly in a pail under the sink. That night, after Kathy passed out, I crouched on the floor to check on them. Even in the dark, I could see them, drifting. It was a safe feeling for me. Kathy snored. Four. Four made a family, wasn't that math?

The next morning I hinged forward over the toilet and waited. It was like my bile was trying to jump up my throat, but was too tired. It was like tryouts for a high jump team. The bile had bright yellow uniforms. Kathy was still asleep on the couch.

"Hello, may I please speak to the person who handles your merchant account?"

"Hello, what is your name? Leslie? Great! My name is Andrea and I'm calling from—"

"We've been mandated by all the major banks and processors—"

"All the major ones, sir."

"Sir, can I—Sir, let me explain the service I am offering!"

The air in the office felt laced with cement. It was heavier and heavier each time I took a breath. I'll be here forever, I thought. I'm becoming part of the building. "New York City!" "New York City!" was all over.

At lunch, I sucked balsamic vinegar off of a long, thin strip of cabbage. Kathy called, saying the problem at her apartment was worse than she thought.

"He'll need another day," she said. "He said he's never seen so many butterflies! He said that he caught them fucking all over my books. Isn't that disgusting?"

"Yeah." I felt my stomach twisting inside of me.

"They probably came in through the toilet. Did you know that when a butterfly is cocooning, it is physically impossible to kill?"

I said that I didn't know that. I didn't know much about butterflies. I had grown up in a butterfly-free province.

Later that day, Daryl called me to his desk for a review. "I don't believe you," he said. I put on headphones and listened to a recording of my own voice.

"New York City, ma'am. Yes, we're a major brokerage." It was somehow both weak and heavy, like something filled with mud.

"I don't believe you work for a major finance company," He said, leaning back in his chair. "I don't believe you even live in New York City. If you want to generate leads, I need you to believe it." Then he closed his eyes, which was how you believed in things.

After work, I joined some of my coworkers in the alley adjacent to our building, where there was a large vent blowing warm air onto the street: ideal for smoking weed. I stood around with them, fidgeting for a spot in the heat. Alex, a senior analyst, talked about how he preferred large volume leads, while Maria preferred smaller volumes, though more of them. I stayed quiet about my leads, having generated zero that day.

It was impossible for the snow to survive underneath the vent. What must have happened was that after business hours, the vent was turned off, so the melted snow froze. There was all of us, five or six, keeping our balance on the ice. I kept bumping into Alex and our parkas crinkled. There was something adult about his acne, although no, I would not have called him an adult. When he asked me if I wanted to come over for something to eat, I suppose I should have known what was going to happen next.

He did not live far, and once we were inside we sat together on the couch. I tried to remember if we were friends or not, if we had been friendly in the past, so maybe it was not so strange that I was here now, with him, on this lumpy futon in his dirty apartment. But I was stoned and I didn't remember the regular rules for how to be. I wondered, what would Joey do? Although that was a dangerous road to go down.

I didn't want to go home. I didn't want to see Kathy and have her ask me again about him. I hated that I'd told her whatever I'd told her the night before, which I couldn't remember. I could only remember vaguely checking on the turtles: the father, the mother, the older brother and the sister. Four made a family, wasn't that math?

Alex pressed his body up to mine and we kissed. It had been so long since I'd had sex that I wasn't exactly sure what I was supposed to do. Then he laid me down without my jacket and I remembered, oh yeah, I'm the girl, I don't have to do anything.

All of this time I'd been trying not the think of the turtles so much. I thought that if I didn't think about them so much, then they wouldn't be so important to me and I wouldn't have to harbour them illegally in my apartment. Because it was a foolish risk and I knew that. But I told myself that if I was doing something else while I was thinking about the turtles, then perhaps the level of harm would not be so bad. So as this strange boy touched me, I retreated into myself and thought of everything I remembered: standing over the basin, watching them drift to and from each other in the water. Maybe, I'd think, these are the years where the little sister wanted to do everything the big brother did. And she followed him around all the time, which I could see with my own eyes, she did. Maybe in her head she pictured him as Prime Minister and herself as President, which little sisters sometimes did. I knew from experience.

They were graceful. Without their shells, the turtles moved like ribbons in the breeze, like a wind puppet, something to be kept on a porch. Their skin was covered in tiny, tiny lines. I thought about how without their wrinkles and their skin stretched out to its fullest potential, they'd probably be one hundred times their size and impossible to fit inside of my tiny, dirty apartment. I thought they looked either like babies or a hundred years old. Maybe these were the years later, when they told the little sister how strange the brother was, and how she should spend more time with her own friends, not realizing that they were all strange. They were all actually tiny turtles I'd found in my apartment.

Soon enough we got to the point that I always get to with sex, when the sensation of his dick moving in and out of me stops feeling like anything, like my body has simply acclimatized to his dick. "You're so hot," he said.

When we finished, I got up to use the washroom. In the mirror was my face, although I didn't care. It could have been anyone's.

· On the bottom of the medicine cabinet was a thin row of cocoons. I bent over to look closely, their thin green layers. Growing up, I'd been afraid of butterflies, hearing horror stories of infestations in people's cabins, how they'd open rice bags to find hundreds of them, bursting out like a flame. They said that in San Francisco there were butterflies the size of human palms. But I didn't care. They quivered just from my breath so close to them. I could have been covered in them and I wouldn't have cared.

I walked out of his apartment and onto the street. I did not want to go home. I walked into the university campus, then turned around again and back towards the closed, glowing stores. I walked past so many people and none of them even knew Joey. Even if I told them all about him, I'd probably always be forgetting something, like the time he set the garbage can on fire or how he sucked all the ink out of a grape-flavoured marker, and then never ate a single grape again. He hated them. He hated most fruits. All vegetables. He hated television. He hated our dad who he called "the fag" and he said I was a fag, too. I told him that if he didn't hang out with me, then I'd tell mom and dad about whatever I found in his room. So sometimes in the evenings, we'd sit on the back porch together, talking about how we hated our town. He'd say, "Ok, that's enough, it's been fifteen minutes," and he'd look into the sun, I thought he could read the sun.

I'd say, "No, but that was a lot of weed," which it always was. So he'd sit back down and say who was a freak and who was retarded.

Walking: This was how I imagined Joey to be, walking somewhere with a purpose. When my parents sat me down to say that he was missing, it was so exciting. He must have gone somewhere fantastic, I thought. Even when you are from where we were from, you knew the world had vast and splendid offerings.

"We don't know where he is," my father had said, slowly as if it was something difficult to understand. Well, of course, I thought, all you know is the mall, the rink, our basement. Even then I thought of New York City, in the night or the way home from school: how bright it would be, how exciting. I'd be part of it too, I'd become a piece of the lights.

And it was not until I walked into my bedroom and saw the wooden box with the red-eyed dragon carved into its lid that I knew how much I'd misunderstood. I lifted it open to my nose, inhaling the scent of the stinky moss as my heartbeat began to multiply. He would have taken that wherever he went, though he'd left it for me. But I did not tell anyone. I held the fact inside my stomach for two days until the police officer called to say that some dog from the search party had found Joey in the woods.

Snow leapt into my boots. I knew that when I got home my feet would be wet and white and peeling, so I did not go home for a long time. I walked for so long that I told myself, if this were New York City you'd either be dead or cumming in a TCBY. By the time I finally got to my apartment Kathy was passed out with all the lights on and a third bottle of wine empty on the coffee table.

I knelt down in front of the sink, opening the cupboard door. Inside, without the wind, my skin was still my skin but I smelt like the boy, thick and salty. Kathy said something in her sleep, something that sounded like, "*cheeeese.*"

The town where I grew up was divided by a river. If you followed the river east, you'd find the mall and if you followed it west, you'd find my high school. Every so often a famous hockey player grew out of our rinks and you'd hear girls bragging about how he'd fingered them. Plaques were pressed. Kathy wasn't from this town, but the next one over, where people thought they were better but secretly weren't.

I remembered that one summer she was staying with us because her mother had to travel for her new boyfriend's work. Kathy was with me in the backyard, and I was introducing her to some of my stuffed animals when Joey ran down from the treehouse with scabbed knees and his penis out. He stood right in front of us and wagged it back and forth, trying to catch both of us right in the eyes. When he laughed Kathy began to cry. She ran inside, kicking all of my toys into the dirt. My mother called for us.

"Kathy is lying," I said, "she's making it up." My mother looked down at each of us. This was so long ago, when Joey was nine and Kathy and I were six. It was before he had really become Joey—the one who sold weed and threatened to fuck teachers and drove drunk into the shut down Arby's so bad he broke his leg at an angle the doctor's said he'd never walk straight again—so my mother believed me.

"Upstairs," she said to Kathy, which was where Kathy stayed for the rest of the day. Later, in the evening, I walked into her room where she sat on the floor, playing with a doll she had packed from home. "Maybe you wanted to see it," I said, "maybe that's why you made it up." She was, after all, the girl whose mother didn't want her, not for an entire summer, and all because she was dating a roadie for Soundgarden. But my words meant nothing, Kathy didn't listen. She only sat there, braiding and unbraiding hair.

I walked with the pail into my bedroom. On the floor next to my bed, I watched each tiny turtle and began to think about all the things that had happened to me as a kid and it made me so sick to think that they will always have happened to me, no matter what I did. His room always felt warmer than the rest of the house, but that might have just been the smell. It was always a great adventure, tiptoeing through his dirty clothing in search of a clear floor. I hated that I remembered this feeling and told myself that I didn't really remember it. It's not really what the floor was like, you're thinking of the floor somewhere else and you're conflating those memories to feel sorry for yourself.

"You're my infestationable beings," I said to the turtles, slight as fingers drifting in the tap water. Sometimes I wondered if it really was the father who had the shell. Maybe, I thought, it was the little girl and that made her the strongest one of all.

The turtles moved slowly, as if the water was thick, and then I noticed one of them wasn't moving at all. My heart beat begun to multiply. I touched the turtle with my fingers but my hands shook so much that the water spilt all over me, onto my thighs, onto the floor. I held it in my palm, its smooth, raw back against my palm and other turtles looked up, out of the water and right into my eyes. I understood. He was the older brother. First to go is always the older brother, I said to the turtles, and then I started thinking all that's probably happened is that he'd simply had enough and one day went walking in the woods by the river to search for the tallest tree he could find. And he climbed to the top, tied himself to its trunk, looked out across the valley, then flew away.

"Why do you have to be so typical?" I said to the tiny turtle. "Why do you have to be like every brother I know?"

I dropped him into the toilet and the water splashed onto my knees. I pressed the handle and the turtle spun in smaller and smaller circles, like I said, eventually disappearing from me forever and of course it was not long after this that each one died

Nobody believed me. Nobody believed I could live in New York City. I did not work at the call centre long after this, I did not work there for very long at all. However, for some reason this time period still features prominently in my memory. Sitting on the bathroom floor like that, after the bowl had emptied and then refilled with fresh water, I was looking from the top to bottom of it, wondering what I was looking for. I was thinking, if a butterfly was going to be a butterfly and there was literally nothing in the world that can stop it, what then, is going to happen to me?

A Plot of Ocean

Hillary and Angela were in the corner, folding napkins into shapes that looked like vaginas.

"So how long have you been in Australia?" asked Hillary. Hillary was broad, taller than Angela, with her hair pulled back into a low ponytail.

"About two months. You?" Angela was slim and petite. She had a round face with large, wide-set eyes. They looked nothing alike, although probably to a lot of the other caterers from Pinnacle they could have been twins. They had exactly the same complexion. Both of their faces had gone red carrying the ice buckets.

"I just got here," said Hillary, "a week ago. I'm going to save up money for a van and drive to Byron Bay. You should come."

"Cool," said Angela.

They were both in uniform: starched white shirts, striped ties and black trousers. It was their second shift working a banquet together. Every week the caterers, mostly backpackers, called Pinnacle Headquarters on Flinders Street and the agents gave them shifts. Angela had been working all week and she had another shift the next morning, even though the dinner service wouldn't end until after one.

Yuko called them for the main. Each caterer retrieved plates, either meat or vegetarian, from the festering chefs and followed Yuko out into the massive banquet hall, past the stage and among the wealthy guests, dressed in their finest.

The plates were heavy, especially when you carried three at a time. They had to be balanced or else the sauce would spill everywhere and the integrity of the dish's presentation would be ruined. Once Angela had spilt sauce onto her wrist, staining her white shirt. Yuko had seen and screamed at her.

Angela marched with the rest of the caterers, mostly Italian, German and Korean. When she was about halfway to Yuko the sight caught her, out of the corner of her eye. It looked just like...but it couldn't be. She thought she had seen her baby, but that was impossible. *That's not my baby*, she thought, *it can't be*. Her baby had come at the wrong time in her life and had to be gotten rid of. There was no way it could be here now, eating dinner in Melbourne.

She dropped off her plates at sixty, then marched back to the kitchen to pick up another round.

"Hurry, hurry, faster, faster!" The chefs were throwing garnishes onto the plates and dripping sweat into the sauce. "Hurry the fuck up!" They were so angry.

"Come on sweetheart," one of the chefs said bitterly to Angela.

"You ok?" Hillary, who was carrying the vegetarian option, asked her.

There it was again. It was definitely the baby, even from far away that was something Angela knew in her gut and the hairs on the back of her neck agreed. What was it doing here, now? Angela was trying to work.

Now the baby was talking to someone else at another table. What was it saying? Was it talking about her? Well, what else did the baby know about? It had been inside of her for a few months and that was it. It was probably telling the other guests about how Angela had dreamt of becoming a set designer, but that the only set she'd ever designed had been for a play that tanked. And she didn't even get accepted into the set design program at the university. After that, she got so lost about her life that she flew across the world, pretty much on a whim. The baby and the guests were laughing at her. Jesus Christ. It was sitting right where Yuko was directing Angela to serve her plates.

"Fifty-two, fifty-two," Yuko was yelling at the caterers. She could scream at the top of her lungs and none of the guests would notice, the sounds of their chatter were that engaging. Later there would be a band and speeches. Fifty-three was where the baby sat.

If Angela had to serve her own baby, she would die. It would be so awkward she'd pass out and the plates would fall, breaking on the ground. The food would fall all over her and she'd pee her pants. Everyone would see. She'd wake up and everyone would be staring at her with Yuko yelling table numbers, "fifty-six, forty-two, eleven, three!"

But when she got to the table, the baby was gone. It must have slipped away.

After the service was over, Hillary asked Angela if she wanted to grab a beer. They walked in their undershirts through the dark streets. "I think there's a bar over here," one of them would say, but the bars were always full. No one is going to want us with our backpacks anyways, Angela thought, though her sleek, leather backpack was much nicer than Hillary's bulky MEC.

Finally they found a bar through an alley. Angela had been there before on a date, with someone from Ontario who she had met through Pinnacle, but all he wanted to talk about was Canada. "Did you hear about the new Cabinet Minister?" "Did you read about the woman murdered in Lacombe?"

The bar was nearly empty. A few men nursed beers by the counter and a couple sat in the back, kissing.

Hillary asked Angela if she had ever been to the Dominican Republic. Angela had not.

"I love the DR," she said, "my ex was from there. He was so hot. The first time we had sex it was bad, because his dick was too big."

"Crazy," said Angela. "Awesome."

A man walked over to them and introduced himself as Carl. He was older than them, but probably only by a few years. He had curly hair.

The girls explained how they were from Canada and had spent the evening serving dinner at the convention centre.

"Wow," he said, "Canada."

"They have the worst cover bands," Angela began, describing their shifts. "They play Black Eyed Peas, that song from *The Muppets*."

"That 'We Are A Family' song," said Hillary.

He was staring at Angela. "Do you like catering?"

"No," she burst out laughing.

"Would you like another drink?"

He knew of a bar, which had more going on that this one did.

"All of the bars are full," said Hillary, though it was beginning to have nothing to do with her.

"I know someone," said Carl, absent-mindedly playing with their shot glasses.

As they walked out and into the alley Hillary whispered to Angela, "I'd be careful. This guy creeps me out."

"I know," said Angela, "but I don't want to go home yet."

Carl paid for the three of them to get into the next bar without waiting in line. It was loud and crowded. From the corner of her eye, Angela thought she saw the baby again, though when she turned to look, it was only a woman's thigh, fleshy and wide as she danced against a pool table.

Very quickly Hillary got caught in a booth, talking to a boy. "Do you like him?" Angela asked when she got back from the bar with Carl and a drink.

"Oh, she likes him," said Carl, "I can tell."

"He's a boy," Hillary said. "And I'm only into men."

Carl wanted to have a cigarette, so the three of them walked out to the patio, which was just as crowded, but cooler. Some people were backpackers, pointing up at what might have been the Southern Cross in the sky. Really you had to go out of the city to see the real sky, many people had told Angela, but she had not yet had the chance.

"What is this effect you have on men?" Carl asked her. "You're so beautiful."

"Are you drunk?" Hillary asked from the other side of her.

"No," said Angela, though it was becoming difficult to finish her drink. The beer was becoming heavy, like a sludge. "I'm fine." She started to laugh. "Are you drunk?"

"It takes a lot to get me drunk," Hillary said.

"I mean it," Carl continued. "I knew it, the bartender at the last bar knew it. I said to him, 'Are there any girls I should talk to?' He said, 'over there, the brunette with her back to you.'"

"I don't know," said Angela, laughing. She could not quite wrap her head around this baby business. Why was it here and what did it want from her? It had been almost a year since she'd thought about it in any significant way. Several months, at least. Her life had moved on.

After a little while, Hillary said that she was going home and asked Angela if she wanted to come with her. Angela said no, she didn't want to go home yet.

"Are you going to be ok?"

"Yeah."

"How are you getting home?"

"I'll cab," said Angela.

"Do you have money?"

"Yeah," she said, although she didn't. Cabs were expensive, she never would, she couldn't.

"Here," Hillary pulled out a bright bill.

"No really, I'm fine."

"Have a good time."

"I'll see you around Pinnacle," Angela said, hiccupping.

They had one more drink and then Carl leaned into Angela and said, "I want to get out of here." When they were out on the street, he propelled past her, onto the road, hailing a cab.

"Alright mate?" a group of men asked him. He tripped over the curb.

"Your boyfriend is drunk," the men told Angela.

"She's not my girlfriend," Carl said and the men hollered. Carl curled into himself and threw up into his palm, then dropped the sick onto Bourke Street.

The cab winded into what Angela supposed was St. Kilda, where he had told her he lived, though she didn't know, she'd never been. All she did since arriving in Melbourne was cater and go on dates.

He showed her his bedroom and Angela saw a photograph of him holding a woman with blonde hair in front of The Twelve Apostles.

"Is that your girlfriend?"

Carl lay face down on the bed and groaned into the blankets. "Yes," he said, "but we can't be together." So they weren't going to have sex, Angela felt relieved. Perhaps it had been obvious for some time.

"Why?" she asked.

"Because she's a Mormon and she hates how much I drink. I said I'd be a Mormon too, but I'm not good enough for her. No matter what I do, if I'm sober, if I'm a Mormon."

Angela asked him if he'd like a glass of water. But he was already asleep and snoring.

She slept beside him in the bed. In the morning she opened and smelled each girl product in the shower. They smelt like candles. She looked at herself in the mirror. She really was beautiful, she had an effect on men. Her back in this lighting was phenomenal. What if she wrote down her number and left it for Carl beside his bed? Would he quit drinking for her as well? What if she asked him? It was nine a.m. She had to be at the convention centre in fifteen minutes if she wanted to make check-in to facilitate the breakfast buffet. But she didn't want to. She left the apartment building and started walking.

She followed the bigger and bigger houses, down towards the beach. When she got to the palm trees, she took off her shoes and socks.

There, in the sand in front of her, was the baby.

"Are you surprised to see me?" it asked.

"No," she said, after thinking about it for a little while. Even though she had been so shocked the night before, she said, "I think I knew I would see you. I've thought about you a lot."

"Really?" asked the baby.

"Sort of," she said. She knew she wasn't supposed to. She knew she was supposed to have moved on.

There were other people on the beach, though it felt to Angela that her and the baby were the only things to have ever happened in the whole world.

"So what have you been up to?" asked the baby. "Are you still designing sets?"

She shook her head. "Not really. It was just the one."

"You wanted to design sets for a living," the baby said. "You used to say you wanted to design sets for Broadway."

"No, that wasn't serious."

"You used to talk about it all the time."

"No." She felt humiliated by remembering, it was such a joke. "I was probably just joking."

"So what are you doing here, in Australia?"

She didn't know.

The baby smirked. "So you're not doing anything?"

"Well, what are you doing?"

"I'm a baby. Or at least, I'm trying to be."

They walked silently into the shade of a high-rise and sat down. There should have been lots to talk about, but Angela couldn't think of anything to say and after a while no longer tried to. She was relaxed and pushed sand through her fingers.

"Do you know any Mormons?" she asked the baby, finally.

The baby scoffed, "I don't know anyone." It seemed to be getting testy, angry about how it had never had a life.

"It's not my fault," Angela said, "they told me you would just float around for a while and then go to another family who wanted you. It's not my fault that this turned out to be misinformation."

"Maybe it wasn't," said the baby.

"What do you mean?"

"Nothing."

"You're going to another family?" Angela's pulse began to quicken. The air was so hot, even under the shade.

"Nothing," it said.

"You are!"

The baby turned to her, with its eyes sharp. "It's not another family, as if you were one. It's a *family*. It can't just be two people."

"So you're going?" Now her voice was lower.

"I'm not getting my hopes up."

Angela thought about how the baby had first been taken out of her, when she lay in the medical chair reclined 100% back, staring up at the ceiling where a postcard with a photograph of a beach had been taped. The beach on the postcard was not so unlike the beach they sat on now, as if she had somehow crossed a threshold to exist in the realm of cheap, DIY hospital art.

After the surgery was over, the nurse walked Angela into an adjacent room where a row of girls lay in beds divided by curtains. Each girl wore an identical gown, thin as paper. *But which one of us wears it best?* For a moment, Angela needed to know.

Both Angela and the baby stared into the water. The waves would grow with gentle conviction out of the ocean, reach their peak and then melt into the sand, as though they never existed. New ones who looked just like them, almost exactly, rose and fell in their place.

"What are they like?" Angela asked the baby, referring to the family.

"I don't know," it said. "I'm not getting my hopes up."

"Have you had your hopes up before?" Angela asked.

"You know how it is," the baby said, squinting into the sun.

"I was good you know, I had an understanding of light and texture. Like hanging curtains and stuff. Paul—the director, he told me. He'd worked at the university."

The baby nodded.

"But it just got frustrating." She went on: "All I was doing was designing." She made models for set designs in shoe boxes. "I'd spend a whole day just making chairs out of cardboard. Sometimes I even painted a design on the cardboard, say if the chair was supposed to be from the sixties or seventies. Sometimes the plays I designed for existed, sometimes they didn't. But in the end they were for no one. I just put all the boxes in my parent's garage. A big stack of them, like a cross section of an apartment building."

"I should have been an actress," she said, "but I don't know why I always just wanted to stay in my room folding stuff instead."

Two young people ran into the plot of ocean Angela and the baby had been watching. They started to kiss and the boy snuck his hand into the bottom of the girl's bathing suit, like they were the only two people in the world. *What if the baby left me right now?* Angela thought. What if where the baby went was right in front of her, there in the waves as the boy and girl's toes curled into the sand of deeper and deeper water. The baby would shrink, float through the air and then, as the girl gasped in the arms of the boy, slip down her throat like a pill, rooting itself within her layers. Over time, the baby would have never belonged to Angela in the first place. What if that was how it worked? What if that was the truth? That despite everything Angela knew and had been told, the things she thought had a point to them after all.

Though if it bothered her that much, why didn't she just run back to the apartment where she had slept, ring the bell and say, "I think I left my earrings by the sink," or "My cell phone's on your nightstand, can I just come in for a second?" From which point it would be simple. They'd only have to look at each other, in the specific and shy ways she'd learned from music videos as a teenager. It had worked for Angela before, so it was possibly worth a try now. Even if he spent the whole time pretending she was someone else, that was his right.

Except who wanted to have a baby? All the time and for every day of her life? No, on second thought, she wouldn't want to do that, how monotonous. So then Angela would have to lie back in another chair, maybe with a postcard of the mountains on the ceiling, and come out so screwed up about it that all she'd do for days is watch YouTube videos of "Rihanna's Bitchiest Moments," then finally decide to fly across the world for a second time, ending up exactly where she began.

"Are you doing anything today?" she asked the baby. Maybe if it were free, they could take the train down-town and go to a museum.

The baby shrugged. "Baby stuff," it said.

"Like what?" she asked. What could babies like this one possibly have to do? She imagined a whole herd of them, floating over the glittering ocean. A gang of beiges and browns, just having fun and talking shit about the bodies they had lived inside of.

"You wouldn't get it," the baby said, "you're not a baby."

That was true. She was twenty-four.

It was almost noon. Angela was definitely fired from her job, or she wasn't, and she'd get to serve more rich people meals. But she wanted to keep hanging out with the baby, for just a little bit longer.

"Ok," said the baby, "but I can't stay here forever, I'm going to have to leave at some point."

Acknowledgements

Thank you to Guillaume, Ashley, and Jay.

Thank you to my professors and classmates
at Concordia University.

Thank you to Bükem, Ethel, Dave, Diandre, Halley,
Jon, Julie, Kate, Lizy, Moe, Steff and Thomas.

Thank you to Jacob.

Thank you to my parents.

Frankie Barnet is a Montreal-based writer. Her work has appeared in publications such as Joyland, Lemonhound, and Papirmasse, and she is the author of the 2012 chapbook *Something Disgusting Happening* [Trapshot Archives]. She is a graduate of the Creative Writing program at Concordia University.